Fun in the Mud

by Anna Prokos

illustrated by Dave Clegg

RED
CHAIR
• PRESS •

The sun is rising on the farm.
Time for Rooster to sound the alarm.

"Cock-a-doodle-do! Open your eyes!
Get ready for a big surprise!"

Pig squeals, "It's time to play!
I'm going in the mud today."

Pig races to the squishy mud.
He splashes in with a great big THUD!

"Yahoo!" Pig says. "The mud's all mine!"
Then Goat trots over to join the swine.

"Oh, what fun!" Goat says with glee.
"I've found someone to play with me."

7

Pig looks at Goat and shakes his snout.
"The mud's all mine," Pig says. "Stay out!"

Goat says sadly, "That's not fair!"
He knows that friends should always share.

"Let's take turns," Goat says. "It's fun.
There is lots of mud for everyone."

Just then, Rooster comes strutting through.
He wants to play in the mud too.

"Go away!" Pig says. "The mud's all mine!"
"You're being a hog!" Rooster tells the swine.

Goat says, "The mud will fit us three.
We'll all have fun. Don't you agree?"

Pig thinks. He shouts, "Sure! Come on in!
Now our mud party can begin!"

Splashing and laughing, the three farm friends play in the mud until the day ends!

Big Question: Does Pig have more fun in the mud when he shares with Goat and Rooster? Why?

Big Words:

snout: the nose and mouth of an animal

squeals: makes a loud high-pitched noise

strutting: walking in an upright, confident way